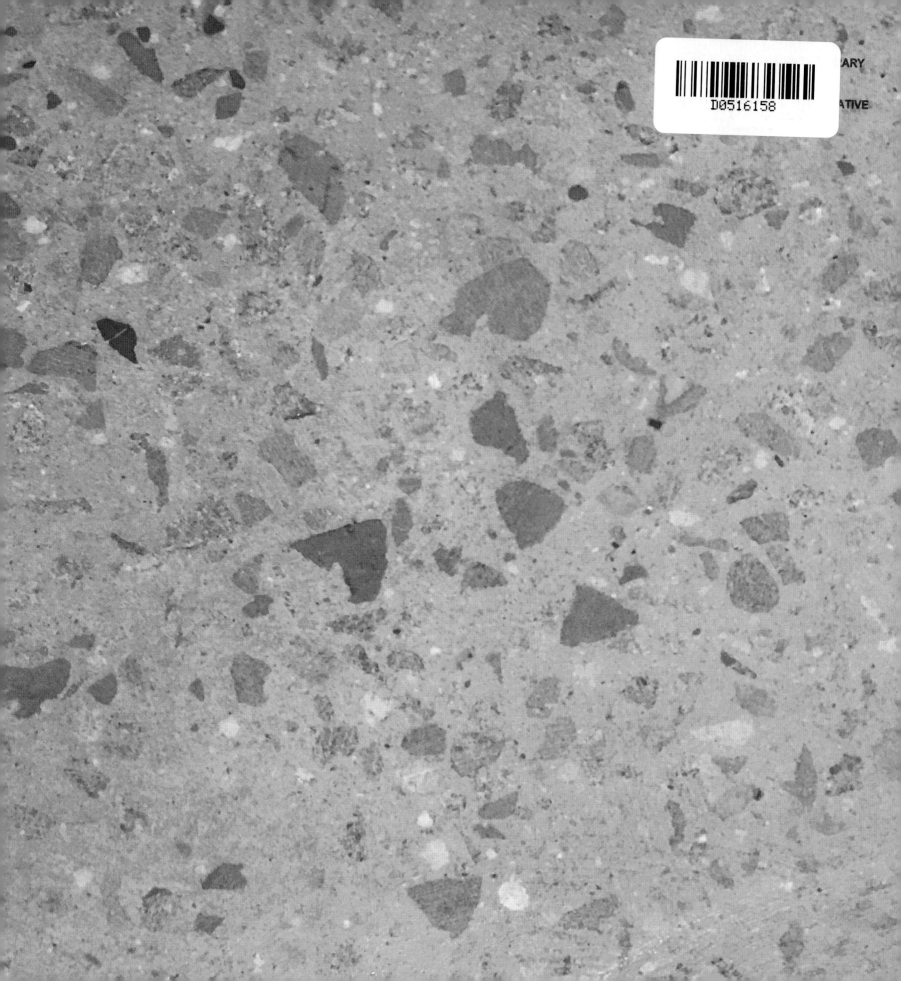

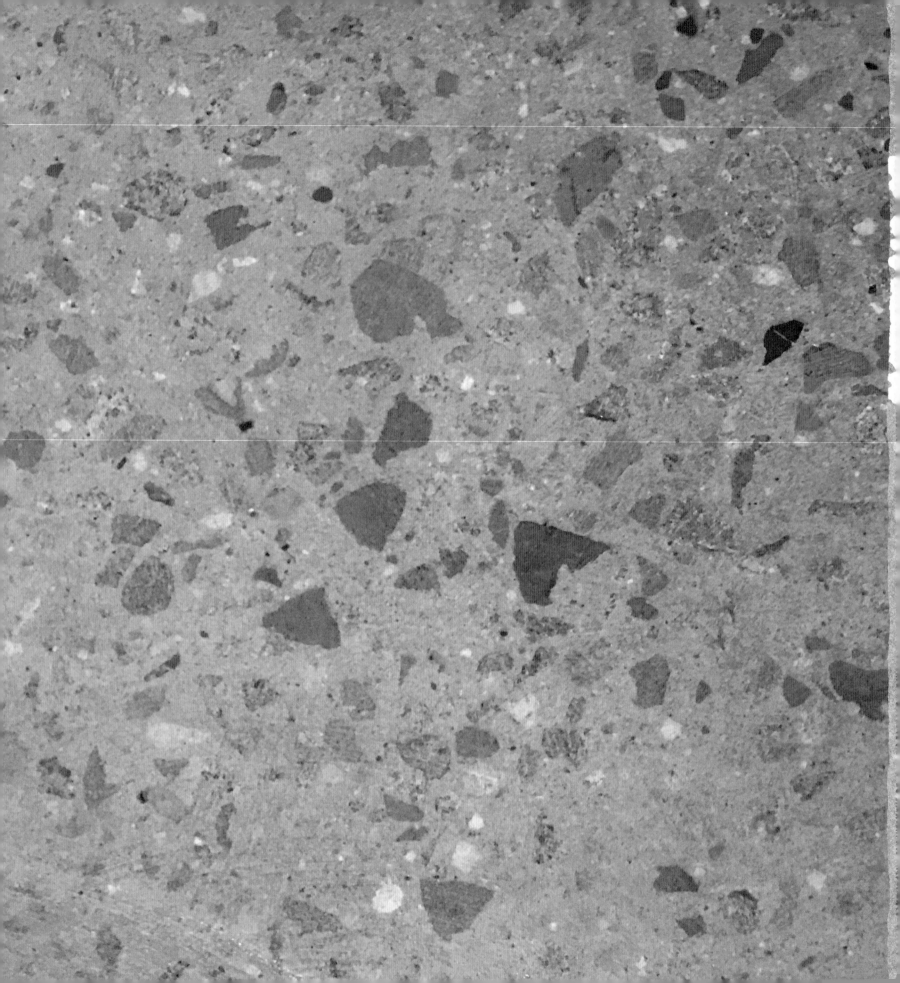

DIG, DUMP, ROLL

For John
S. S.

First U.S. edition 2018

Library of Congress Catalog Card Number pending
ISBN 978-1-5362-0391-2

18 19 20 21 22 23 CCP 10 9 8 7 6 5 4 3 2 1

Printed in Shenzhen, Guangdong, China

This book was typeset in Anton.
The illustrations were done in acrylic inks.

Candlewick Press
99 Dover Street
Somerville, Massachusetts 02144

visit us at www.candlewick.com

DIG, DUMP, ROLL

SALLY SUTTON · ILLUSTRATED BY BRIAN LOVELOCK

CANDLEWICK PRESS

Crash-a-rumble!
Smash-a-grumble!

What's at work?
Here's a clue:

it will

clear the

ground

for you.

Bulldozer!

Coming through!

Bang-a-shudder!
Clang-a-judder!
What's at work?
Here's a clue:

it will
dig big holes
for you.

Digger!
Digger!

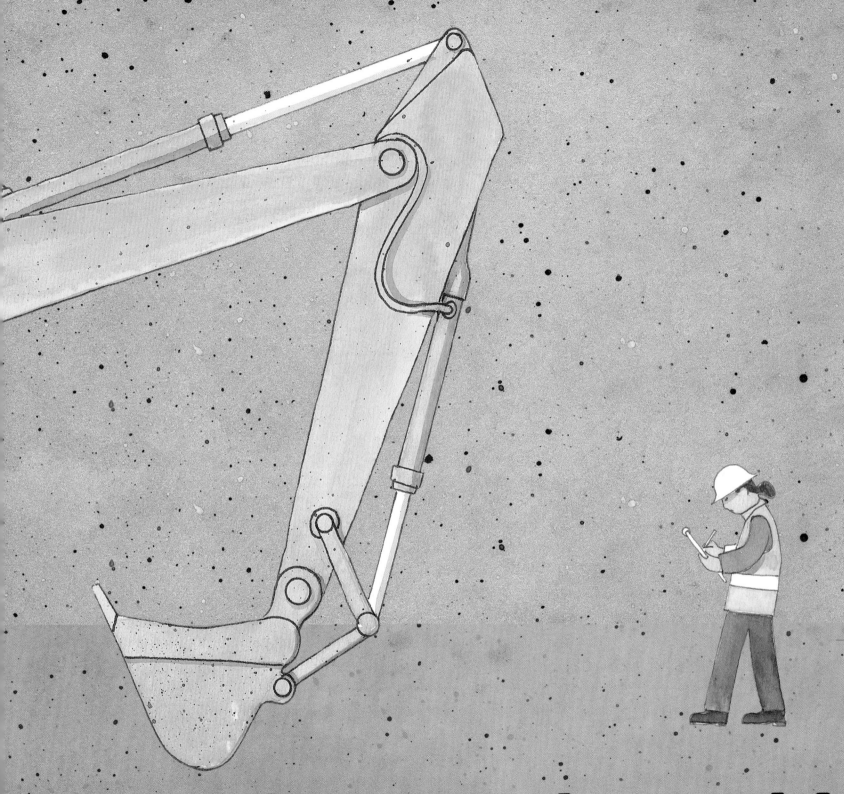

Coming through!

Slam-a-tippa!
Wham-a-slippa!

What's at work?

Here's a clue:

it will

dump out
earth

for you.

Dump truck!

Dump truck!

Coming through!

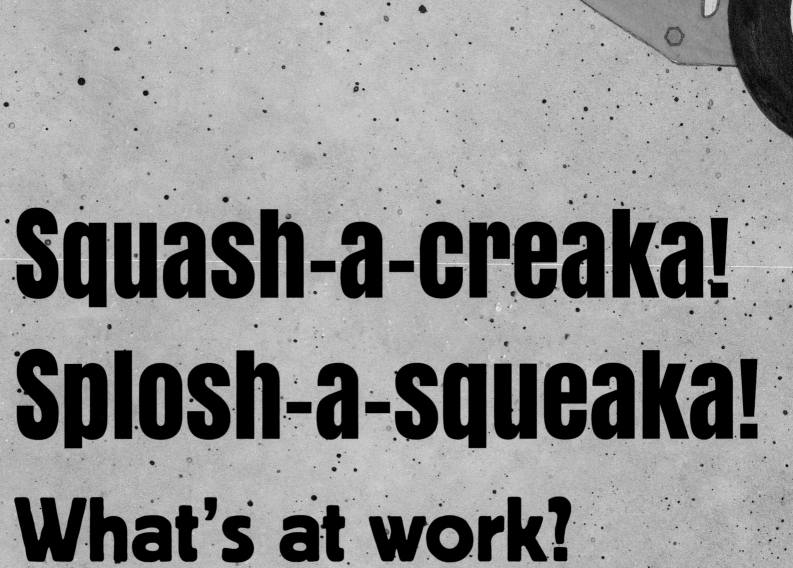

Squash-a-creaka!
Splosh-a-squeaka!
What's at work?
Here's a clue:

it will
**roll the
ground**
for you.

Roller! Roller!

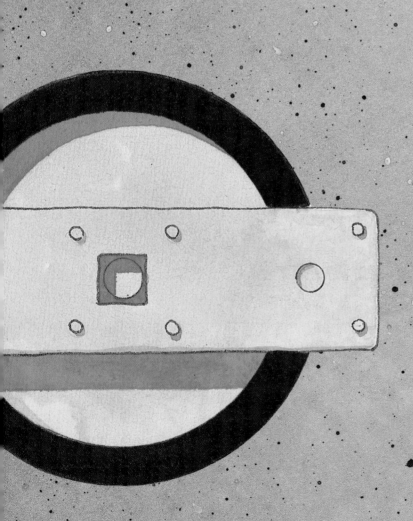

Coming through!

Sploosh-a-splisha! Swoosh-a-swisha!

What's at work?

Here's a clue:

it will
mix cement
for you.

concrete mixer!

Coming through!

Wham-a-hammer!
Bam-a-slammer!
Who's at work?
Here's a clue:

they will
**build a
frame**
for you.

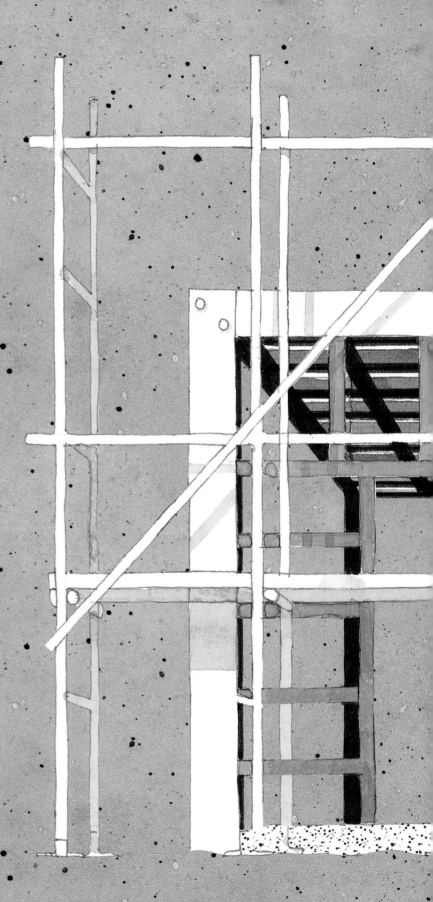

Builders! Builders!

Coming through!

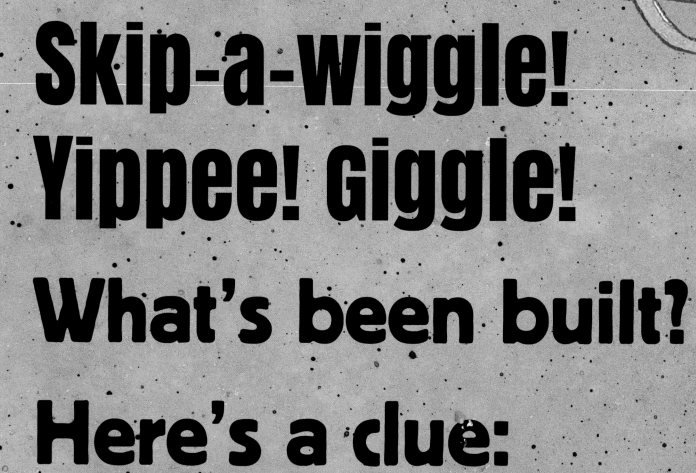

Skip-a-wiggle! Yippee! Giggle!

What's been built? Here's a clue:

you can **learn and play** here too.

School! School!

Just for you!

MACHINE PARTS

DIGGER

Boom

Stick

Bucket

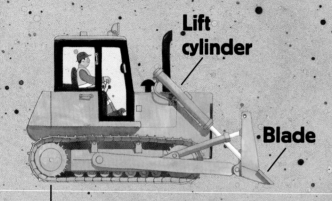

BULLDOZER

Lift cylinder

Blade

Track pad

CONCRETE MIXER

Main chute

Drum

Water tank

DUMP TRUCK

Dump bed

Hoist cylinder

Tailgate

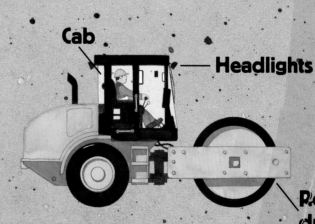

ROLLER

Cab

Headlights

Rolling drum